*All children have
a great ambition to read
to themselves . . .*

*and a sense of achievement when they can do so.
The* **read** **it** **yourself** *series has been devised to
satisfy their ambition. Since many children learn
from the Ladybird Key Words Reading Scheme,
these stories have been based to a large extent
on the Key Words List, and the tales chosen are
those with which children are likely to be familiar.*

*The series can of course be used as
supplementary reading for any reading scheme.
The* Magic Stone *is intended for children
reading up to Book 5c of the Ladybird Reading
Scheme. The following words are additional to
the vocabulary used at that level —*

tramp, woods, tired, day, night, himself,
been, old, woman, world, better, sleep, kind,
went, morning, hungry, think, meal, poor,
garden, turnips, onions, soup, remember,
stone, began, stir, taste, delicious, course,
back, would, beef, barley, if, salt, fit, king,
table, never

*A list of other titles at the same level will be
found on the back cover.*

The Magic Stone

adapted for easy reading by Fran Hunia
from the traditional Swedish tale,
Stone Soup

illustrated by Martin Aitchison

Ladybird Books Loughborough

A tramp was out walking in the woods. The sun was going down and the tramp was getting tired, for he had walked all that day.

"I must look for a house soon, so that I can stop for the night," he said to himself.

He walked on, looking for a house as he went, but all he saw was tree after tree. There was not a house to be seen.

The tramp was about to give up looking for a house and sleep by a tree for the night. Then he looked up and saw an old woman who was out looking for firewood.

He was pleased to see her and
they stopped to talk.

"Good day to you," said the tramp. "What are you doing out here in the woods?"

"I am looking for wood for my fire," said the old woman. "And what about you, my good man? What are you doing here? Where do you come from, and where are you going?"

9

"I have been to see the world," said the tramp, "but now I am tired and I'm looking for a house so that I can stop for the night. I've looked and looked, but I haven't seen a house all afternoon."

"So that's what you want, is it?" said the old woman. "Then you will have to keep on looking. You can't come home with me, and there are no other houses here. You had better be off now, or night will come and you will have to sleep out here in the woods."

The tramp was not going to be put off.

"You look like a kind woman," he said. "I know you will not let me sleep in the woods. Please take me home with you for one night. I'll be off again in the morning, and you will see no more of me."

The tramp went on talking about this and that. Then the old woman said, "You can sleep at my house for one night, but I have no bed for you. You will have to sleep on a chair."

The tramp thanked the old woman, and off they went.

As they walked to the old woman's house, the tramp talked about all the things he had seen. Then he said how tired and hungry he was.

"So you are hungry too, are you?" said the old woman. "But you mustn't think that I can give you a meal. I'm a poor old woman. I haven't eaten all day, and there isn't a thing to eat in my house. You will have to go to sleep hungry, or keep on walking."

They came to the old woman's house. The tramp looked in the garden and saw that the old woman was not as poor or as hungry as she said she was. She had turnips and onions in her garden, and a cow to give her milk.

" This old woman is not as hungry as I am," said the tramp to himself. "I think I know how to make her give me a good meal."

The old woman and the tramp
went into the house.

"So you haven't eaten all day,"
said the tramp. "You must be so
hungry! Sit down and let me make
you some soup."

"Soup?" said the old woman.
"How can you make me some
soup? There isn't a thing to eat in
the house."

"Remember, I have seen the
world, and I can do all kinds of
things," said the tramp. "I know
how to make soup from a stone.
Now what do you think of that?"

"Soup from a stone?" said the old woman. "This I must see! Will you let me look and see how you do it?"

"It was kind of you to take me in for the night, so I will let you see how to make stone soup," said the tramp.

The old woman pulled up a chair and looked on as the tramp put some water on the fire. Then he went out to get a stone from the garden. He put the stone into the water and began to stir. The old woman looked on.

"What will the soup taste like?" asked the old woman.

"Stone soup is delicious," said the tramp. "Of course, it tastes better with an onion or two, but as we have no onions, we will have to make do without them," and he went on stirring the water with the stone in it.

23

The old woman said, "I think I have some onions in my garden. I will go and have a look."

Off she went to look, and soon she was back with two big onions, which she put into the water with the stone.

The tramp stirred and stirred, and the old woman looked on.

"This is going to be good soup," said the tramp. "Of course, it would taste better with a little beef in it, but we have no beef, so we will have to make do without it."

"I think I have a little beef," said the old woman, and off she went to have a look. Soon she was back with some good red beef which she put into the soup with the onions and the stone.

The tramp went on stirring the soup and the old woman looked on.

"This soup is going to be delicious," said the tramp. "Of course, it would taste better with some turnips in it, but as we have no turnips, we will have to make do without them."

"What a good thing it is that I have some turnips in my garden," said the old woman, and off she went to get them. She pulled up two big turnips, then she put them in the soup with the beef, the onions, and the stone.

The soup looked delicious, and
the tramp went on stirring and
stirring. The old woman looked on.

By now the old woman was getting hungry. "That soup looks delicious," she said to the tramp.

"Yes," said the tramp. "Of course, it would be better with some barley in it, but as we have no barley, we will have to make do without it."

"I think I have some barley," said the old woman, and off she went to have a look. Soon she was back with some barley, which she put into the soup with the turnips, the beef, the onions and the stone.

The tramp went on stirring the soup and the old woman looked on. Then the tramp said, " It would be good if we had a little milk to put into our soup, but of course we have no milk, so we will have to make do without it."

"I know what I can do," said the
old woman. "I have a cow out there.
I will go and milk her, and then we
will have some milk for our soup."

The old woman went out to milk the cow. Soon she was back with some milk which she put into the soup with the barley, the turnips, the beef, the onions, and the stone.

Now the soup looked delicious. The tramp went on stirring as the old woman looked on.

The tramp tasted the soup.

"Is it good?" asked the old woman.

"Yes," said the tramp. "All it wants now is some salt and then it will be fit for a king."

"Then I will put some salt in," said the old woman, and off she went to get it.

Soon she was back with some salt which she put into the soup with the barley, the milk, the turnips, the beef, the onions, and the stone. The tramp went on stirring.

"Can we eat the soup now?"
asked the old woman.

"Yes," said the tramp. "Let me
take out the stone, and then we
can sit down and eat soup that is
fit for a king."

" But a king would have other things to eat with the soup," said the old woman, and she put all kinds of delicious things on the table.

" Now there is a meal that is fit for a king," she said.

The tramp said to the old woman, "Now sit down and see what you think of this delicious soup."

The old woman tasted the soup. "Yes, it is delicious," she said, "and to think that you made it from a stone!"

The tramp said, "It was kind of you to take me in for the night, so I am going to give you the stone that made this delicious soup. You will never have to go hungry again."

The old woman was pleased. "Thank you, thank you," she said. "You are the kindest man I know."

Soon the old woman and the
tramp had eaten all the delicious
things. They talked and talked.
Then the old woman said, "I can't
let a kind man like you sleep on a
chair. You must sleep in my bed,
and I will sleep on a chair."

So the tramp went to sleep in the old woman's bed, and the old woman slept on a chair by the fire.

The next day the tramp thanked the old woman for letting him sleep at her house.

"You mustn't thank me," said the old woman. "I am the one who has to thank you, for now that I know how to make stone soup, I will never go hungry again. Do come and see me again some day, and I will make you some delicious stone soup."

"Yes," said the tramp as he walked away. "It is good to know how to make stone soup. But do remember to put in some onions, a little beef, one or two turnips, some barley, and a little milk with the stone. Then stir in some salt and you will have soup that is fit for a king."